# Green Dog

by Melinda Luke
illustrated by Jane Manning

The Kane Press
New York

Acknowledgements: Our thanks to Dr. Robert S. Bandurski, Professor Emeritus of Plant Biochemistry, Michigan State University; Dr. Kathleen Pryer, Assistant Professor, Department of Biology, Duke University; and Marie Long, Reference Librarian, LuEsther T. Mertz Library of the New York Botanical Garden, for helping us make this book as accurate as possible.

Library of Congress Cataloging-in-Publication Data

Luke, Melinda, 1955-
    The green dog / by Melinda Luke; illustrated by Jane Manning.
        p. cm. — (Science solves it!)
Summary: While pet-sitting, Teddy uses science to solve a mystery.
    ISBN: 978-1-57565-115-6 (alk. paper)
    [1. Algae—Fiction. 2. Pet sitting—Fiction. 3. Dogs—Fiction.]
I. Manning, Jane K., ill. II. Title. III. Series.
        PZ7.L97825 Gr 2002
        [Fic]—dc21

                                                        2002000441


eISBN: 978-1-57565-607-6

10 9 8

First published in the United States of America in 2002 by Kane Press, Inc.
Printed at Worzalla Publishing, Stevens Point, WI, U.S.A., October 2014.

Science Solves It! is a registered trademark of Kane Press, Inc.

Book Design/Art Direction: Edward Miller

Visit us online at **www.kanepress.com**

 Like us on Facebook
facebook.com/kanepress

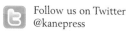 Follow us on Twitter
@kanepress

"Look at that!" I shouted. There was
something at the far end of the lake. It was
green. It was swimming.

My sister, Lizzie, shrieked, "It's a monster!"

"Let's follow it!" yelled my friend Bart.

But the green thing was gone.

"What was that?" asked Lizzie.

"The Monster of Emerald Lake," said Bart in a scary voice.

"Actually, I think it was a dog," I said.

"Oh, Teddy," said Bart, "you've got dogs on the brain."

"That reminds me," I said. "I'd better practice."

I used my best begging voice. "Mom, Dad, may I *please* have a dog?"

"They can't say no to that," said Bart.

But they did.
"A dog needs training," my mom said.
"And care," said my dad.
"Lots of people have dogs," I told them.
"It can't be that hard."
They promised to think it over.

Later on I went back to the lake. I was hoping I'd see that green dog again. Instead I saw Will Roper.

Will was new in town. His job was to make sure the lake was safe for swimming and fishing.

"Hey, Teddy," said Will. "Why so gloomy?"

"I asked my parents for a dog," I explained. "But they think it's too much responsibility."

"Show them you can handle it," said Will.

That night I thought about Will's advice.
Then I had a great idea. I'd look for pet-sitting
jobs. That would show I was responsible!

Teddy Green,
Pet Sitter
VERY
Responsible!

Right away, I got two jobs!
"Feed our goldfish while we go camping,"
said the Novaks.

"Feed my ducklings while I'm on vacation,"
said Mr. Garrett.

I started pet sitting the next day. I even
bought a notebook so I could write down what
I did. Very responsible!

I went to the Novaks' house. Their googly-
eyed goldfish gobbled up the Fancy Fish Flakes
right away.

"It's gloomy in this corner," I told them. "You
need some sun." I moved the goldfish bowl to a
windowsill.

Next I fed Mr. Garrett's ducklings. "You need sun, too!" I said. I moved the umbrella away from their pool. Then I wrote in my notebook.

My first day:
Fed fish.
Put bowl in sun.
Fed ducks.
They quacked.
Moved umbrella.

Every day I fed the goldfish.

Every day I fed
the ducklings.

Every day Bart and I saw the green dog at the far end of the lake. "That dog keeps getting greener," said Bart. "It's weird."

"I'll tell you something just as weird," I said. "The water in the goldfish bowl and the duck pool is green, too!"

"You're kidding!" said Bart. "I'm not," I told him. "But I have an idea."

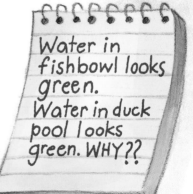

Water in fishbowl looks green. Water in duck pool looks green. WHY??

I got two jars and filled one with water from the goldfish bowl. I even scraped some green stuff from the sides. Bart filled the other jar with water from the duck pool.

Then we took the jars to Will.

"Hey, Teddy. Hey, Bart," said Will. "What are you doing with all that green water?"

"I'm having problems with my pet-sitting jobs," I told him. "These are samples from the goldfish bowl and the duck pool. Could you look at them?"

"Sure," said Will. "We can compare them to some water from the lake."

"The lake water looks kind of green, too,"
I said.

"Do you know why?" asked Will.

"Uh . . . plants?" I guessed.

"I don't see roots or leaves," Bart said.

"You're looking at green algae," said Will.
"They don't have any."

I grabbed my notebook. "How do
you spell that?"

"A-L-G-A-E," said Will. "Here—let's look at your samples under the microscope."

Bart looked first. "Is that ziggy-zaggy stuff green algae?" he asked.

Will checked and said, "It sure is."

Then I looked. I even drew a picture . . .

This is how green algae looks under a microscope.

"What makes this stuff grow?" I asked.

"Food—green algae and green plants make their own," Will said. "They need sunlight to do that."

"Sunlight?" I said. I grabbed my notebook.

My first day:
Fed fish.
Put bowl in sun.
Fed ducks.
They quacked.
Moved umbrella.

18

"I get it!" I said. "The algae grew because I put the fish bowl and duck pool in the sun. What if I put them back in the shade?" I asked.

"You won't have an algae problem," said Will. "But first scrub out the bowl and the pool, and put in clean water."

"Case solved!" Bart said.

"Thanks for telling us all about algae," I said.

Will grinned. "I'm just getting started," he said.

"Uh-oh," I thought. Bart had a "let's go" look on his face.

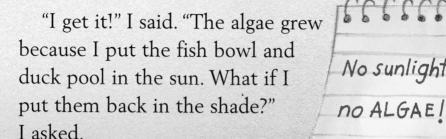

No sunlight, no ALGAE!

But it was too late to leave. Will had pulled out a file marked ALGAE. I got ready to be bored, but it was full of cool stuff.

ZOO MYS...
SOLVED!
Bears White Aga...
Scientists discovered gre...
algae in the polar bear's
fur and in their pool. A salt
mixture was added to the
pool water...

MYSTERY AT THE ZOO!
POLAR BEARS TURN GREEN!
Zoo visitors can't believe their eyes.

Some kinds of algae are as tall as a ten-story building and grow in underwater forests!

Algae grows in surprising places—in waterfalls, even in the desert!

There was even a story about green polar bears. "Hmmm, I wonder . . ."

At that moment there was a scratching noise at the door. It swung open.

**ALGAE** can grow so thick in the Spring and Fall that it looks like a green blanket on the water. Sometimes the blanket is too thick. It cuts off light from the plants below, so they die.

**DID YOU EAT YOUR ALGAE TODAY?**

Most people don't know that algae is in many foods, like ice cream, marshmallows, peanut butter, and jello.

All sea life depends on algae. Tiny creatures eat it. Bigger creatures eat them.

There are thousands of different kinds of algae. Green algae is the most common.

21

"It's the lake monster!" Bart said.

"That's no monster. That's my dog, Molly,"
said Will.

"And she's green from the algae in the lake!"
I said.

22

All living things need food to stay alive . . .

"That's right," said Will.
"Wow," said Bart.
"Cool," I said.

Green algae can make a white dog look green!

23

"Will Molly always be green?" asked Bart.

"No," said Will. "She's about to have puppies. After that, she'll stop swimming for a while and turn into a white dog again."

"But she'll start swimming again," I thought, "and take the family."

Green Puppies!

A few weeks later when I came down to breakfast my mom said, "The Novaks and Mr. Garrett called. They said you're a very responsible pet sitter."

"We're both really proud of you," said Dad.

"Oh, and Will Roper stopped by," Mom added. "He wanted to tell you that Molly was white again. Said you'd understand."

I sure did. Molly must have had her puppies!

"Can I go over to Will's house?" I asked. "Can Bart come with me?"

"Sure," said my parents. "Let's all go."

"Come meet Molly and her pups," said Will.

"Wow," I said. They were the cutest puppies I'd ever seen.

"This one's got your name on it," Will said.

"He's mine?" I asked. I couldn't believe it.
"He is," said my parents.

"He likes you already," said Bart. "What are you going to name him?"

That was easy. "I'm calling him Al," I said. "For ALgae!"

_I can infer!_

# THINK LIKE A SCIENTIST

Teddy thinks like a scientist—and so can you!

You infer all the time. Your dog runs up with a ball in his mouth. So you infer that he wants to play. To infer means that you use what you have noticed, or observed, to help explain how or why something happens.

### Look Back
Look at page 9. Then look at page 13. What does Teddy observe about the water in the goldfish bowl? What does he infer from what he sees? Why?

Answer: Teddy notices that the water is turning green. He knows that the water was clear when he started his job. So he infers that something is probably wrong with the water.

### Try This!
What can you infer from looking at each picture?

| 1. | 2. | 3. |
|---|---|---|

Answer: 1. The dog is hungry or thirsty.
2. The boy probably has been out in the rain.
3. The girl is probably going to a birthday party.